Spooky Bunny Tales

Grosset & Dunlap
An Imprint of Penguin Group (USA) Inc.

GROSSET & DUNLAP
Published by the Penguin Group
Penguin Group (USA) Inc., 375 Hudson Street, New York, New York 10014, USA
Penguin Group (Canada), 90 Eglinton Avenue East, Suite 700,
Toronto, Ontario M4P 2Y3, Canada
(a division of Pearson Penguin Canada Inc.)
Penguin Books Ltd., 80 Strand, London WC2R 0RL, England
Penguin Group Ireland, 25 St. Stephen's Green, Dublin 2, Ireland
(a division of Penguin Books Ltd.)
Penguin Group (Australia), 250 Camberwell Road, Camberwell, Victoria 3124, Australia
(a division of Pearson Australia Group Pty. Ltd.)
Penguin Books India Pvt. Ltd., 11 Community Centre, Panchsheel Park,
New Delhi—110 017, India
Penguin Group (NZ), 67 Apollo Drive, Rosedale, Auckland 0632, New Zealand
(a division of Pearson New Zealand Ltd.)
Penguin Books (South Africa) (Pty.) Ltd., 24 Sturdee Avenue,
Rosebank, Johannesburg 2196, South Africa

Penguin Books Ltd., Registered Offices:
80 Strand, London WC2R 0RL, England

Based upon the animated series *Max & Ruby*
A Nelvana Limited production © 2002–2003.

Max & Ruby™ and © Rosemary Wells. Licensed by Nelvana Limited NELVANA™ Nelvana Limited. CORUS™ Corus Entertainment Inc.
All Rights Reserved. Used under license by Penguin Young Readers Group. Published in 2012 by Grosset & Dunlap, a division of Penguin
Young Readers Group, 345 Hudson Street, New York, New York 10014. GROSSET & DUNLAP is a trademark of Penguin Group (USA) Inc.
Manufactured in China.

ISBN 978-0-448-45864-9   10 9 8 7 6 5 4 3 2 1

The Blue Tarantula

Max wanted his sister, Ruby, to read him a tarantula story before bedtime.

"Let's try a different story, Max," said Ruby. "The tarantula story is too scary."

"Tarantula!" said Max.
"Okay, Max," said Ruby.

But the tarantula story was so scary that Max hid under his blanket.

"Don't worry, Max," said Ruby. "There aren't any tarantulas in your room."

Max was still scared.
"Here's your red rubber elephant, Max," said Ruby.
"Now you can sleep."

"Good night, Max," said Ruby.

Max held his red rubber elephant tight. But he was sure he could hear tarantulas moving around in the closet. "Ruby!" said Max.

Ruby came into Max's room.
"Tarantula!" said Max.
"Where?" asked Ruby.
"Closet! Under bed!" said Max.

Ruby looked around Max's room. There were no tarantulas.

But under Max's bed, Ruby found a jack-in-the-box. "See, Max? It was just a toy making noise," said Ruby. "There are no tarantulas in your room. I'm going back to bed now. Good night, Max!"

Max had an idea. He wound up his lobster toy and let it go. It headed toward Ruby's room.

Ruby heard a noise and sat up in her bed.
"Oh no!" she said. "It must be a tarantula!"

Ruby got out of bed and ran to Max's room.

She jumped into Max's bed.
"There's a tarantula out there!" said Ruby.
"Lobster," said Max, and he went to sleep.

Max's Jack-o'-Lantern

It was Halloween. Grandma came over to help
Max and Ruby prepare for a party. She brought
Halloween treats.

Ruby was putting up decorations.
"Scary, scary!" said Max.
"No, Max," said Ruby. "We want to put up happy decorations. Not scary ones!"

Ruby sent Max upstairs for more decorations.

Max found a box of decorations. But he thought the decorations were too happy. He went in his room and got his rubber spiders.

"Max!" said Ruby. "We don't want spiders at a happy Halloween party. They're too scary! Can you please put them back upstairs?"

Then Ruby asked Max to draw a jack-o'-lantern's face on a pumpkin.

"Make sure it's a happy smiley face, Max," said Ruby. "We don't want a scary-looking pumpkin."

Max drew the best jack-o'-lantern face he could.

He brought it to Grandma in the kitchen. Grandma was baking Halloween cookies. She liked Max's jack-o'-lantern face.

"Wonderful, Max," said Grandma. "Such a smiling jack-o'-lantern! You scoop out the pumpkin, and I'll copy the face on the outside."

Max watched his drawing go onto the pumpkin.
Then Grandma carved the pumpkin.

27

When no one was looking, Max turned the pumpkin upside down.
The happy face became a scary face!

Soon everything was ready for the party.

The guests arrived. "Happy Halloween!" they said. "Happy Halloween!" said Ruby. "Everything at our party is happy!"

"But look!" said the guests. "That pumpkin is not happy at all."

"Scary pumpkin!" said Max.

Ghost Bunny

It was campout night for Ruby's Bunny Scout troop.
"Let's tell ghost stories," said Ruby.
Max wanted to listen.

"Max, ghost stories are too scary for little bunnies," said Ruby. "Why don't you go to sleep in your sleeping bag? We won't be far away."

"This way, you'll be close by," said Ruby. "But you won't be scared by the stories."

Ruby walked back to the Bunny Scouts. Valerie started to tell a ghost story.

But Max heard the story. He walked over to where Ruby and her friends were sitting.
"Ghost! Scary!" said Max.

"There are no such things as ghosts, Max," said Ruby.
"Here are your sleepy-time toys. Now go to sleep. We're
right here, so there's no need to be afraid."

When Ruby rejoined the Bunny Scouts, Valerie began her story again.

But Max could still hear the story, and he was scared.

He walked over to Ruby and the Bunny Scouts.
"Ghost!" said Max.

"Max, there are no ghosts," said Ruby. She walked him back to his sleeping bag.

"Here is your favorite book and a flashlight so you can see. We're right here, so there's no need to be afraid."

Ruby went back to the story circle.
Valerie began her ghost story again.

Max was using his flashlight to read his book.
Then he had an idea.

Suddenly Ruby and the scouts heard a ghostlike noise near the tent.

They saw a shadow dancing on the tent.
"It's a ghost!" said Valerie. "A real ghost! I'm scared!"
"So are we!" said the other scouts.

But the ghost began to giggle.
"Ghost bunny!" said Max.